DISNEP
PIRATES of the CARIBBEAN
JACK SPARROW

The Timekeeper

by Rob Kidd
Illustrated by Jean-Paul Orpinas

Based on the earlier life of the character, Jack Sparrow,
created for the theatrical motion picture,
"Pirates of the Caribbean: The Curse of the Black Pearl"
Screen Story by Ted Elliott & Terry Rossio and Stuart Beattie and Jay Wolpert,
Screenplay by Ted Elliott & Terry Rossio,
and characters created for the theatrical motion pictures
"Pirates of the Caribbean: Dead Man's Chest" and
"Pirates of the Caribbean: At World's End"
written by Ted Elliott & Terry Rossio

DISNEP PRESS

New York

Special thanks to
Rich Thomas and Ken Becker

Copyright © 2007 Disney Enterprises, Inc.

Printed in the United States of America

First Edition
1 3 5 7 9 10 8 6 4 2

Library of Congress Catalog Card Number: 2006909219

ISBN-13: 978-1-4231-0366-0
ISBN-10: 1-4231-0366-1

DisneyPirates.Com

BEAN

JACK SPARROW

The Timekeeper

CHAPTER ONE

Jack Sparrow thought he had seen it all. Mermaids, cursed pirates, swords that could be used to resurrect conquistadors, women who turned into snakes, amulets that turned objects into precious metal—these were all things Jack had become familiar with since he first set sail from the pirate town of Tortuga. From there, he had set off for freedom and adventure aboard the fishing boat he thought of as a ship, the *Barnacle*.

But what now stood not twelve feet from

Jack was unlike anything the young sailor had ever encountered.

Because standing not twelve feet away from Jack was the most feared, treacherous, terrible monster on the Seven Seas—the cursed captain of the *Flying Dutchman*, Davy Jones.

Legend had it that Jones was once an ordinary man. Then, he was charged with the task of ferrying the souls of sailors who'd perished at sea to the next world—an honorable duty. But something went terribly wrong. Jones was deserted by the woman he loved, and the grief that followed was unbearable. He tore his still-beating heart from his body and locked it away in a chest, along with precious mementos of his lost love. Soon, his body began to transform into something more suited to his now-heartless state. His face became monstrous, with tentacles dangling from his cheeks, and the rear of his skull grew to resemble the pulsing body of a large octopus. His hands were replaced by a huge eel-like tentacle and a monstrous claw.

His ship, the majestic *Flying Dutchman*, was also transformed. The entire vessel became covered in an oceanic crust. Barnacles, sea slime, and coral covered the corroded deck. The ship became laden with the bodies of dead sailors, and they began to comprise its hull.

The *Dutchman*'s sails caught wind better than any ship on the seas. And she had the uncanny ability to sail underwater, emerging as if from nowhere alongside an unsuspecting vessel.

Worst of all, the *Dutchman* no longer brought souls to a final resting place as was her original charge. With her unnatural speed and crew, Jones now used the ship to *enslave* sailors. When a seaman met his end, Jones would appear, telling him he could either die or live forever by giving his soul over to Jones. If the sailor chose the latter, then he would become a member of the crew.

Like their captain, the *Dutchman*'s crew had mutated from human to beast. Ultimately, the sailors became a part of the *Dutchman* itself, blending into the very wood of the masts, the decks, and the broadsides, losing all humanity.

And, if a sailor chose death over service? The outcome was no less painful. Jones was master of a realm called Davy Jones's Locker, a nightmarish place where the souls of sailors suffered for all eternity. He had sent many sailors there, and the legends all claimed that no one had ever returned.

As if the ship, the crew, the Locker, and the disembodied beating heart were not bad enough, Jones also had a pet called the Kraken. This giant, squidlike leviathan was capable of terrible acts of destruction, had the foulest breath known to man, and had helped send countless sailors to the Locker.

All these terrible legends, awful tales, horrifying anecdotes, and yet, Jack Sparrow still found it within himself to laugh. In truth it did seem quite ridiculous that the horrible, terrible, awful Davy Jones had just landed on board the *Barnacle* looking for, of all things, a pocket watch.

"Do not toy with me, Sparrow," Jones snarled. "Hand over the watch."

"Pardon me, Mister Jones . . . mind if I call you Davy? Thank you kindly. What in the Seven Seas could you possibly want this piece of pawnshop trash for?" Jack asked, dangling the timepiece that belonged to his only crewmember,* the aristocrat Fitzwilliam P. Dalton III.

Standing close by, Fitzwilliam himself let out a sigh. He had only very recently recovered the watch, which had been given to him by his sister and was stolen from him by a thief months ago.

Though he knew all the stories of Jones and was therefore thoroughly terrified, Fitzwilliam set his square jaw and worked hard to steady his legs and keep a cool demeanor.

"Trash?" Jones said. "The only trash I see here are two little boys lost at sea, and a pathetic excuse for a seaworthy vessel!"

"Hold it there, mate," Jack said defensively. "This is *my* pathetic excuse for a

*The rest of his crew—Arabella, Jean, Tumen, Tim, and even pesky old Constance ditched Jack to sail aboard the *Fleur de la Mort* in Vol. 7, *City of Gold*

seaworthy vessel, and you're standing aboard it, so you might want to show it, and me, her *captain*, some respect."

Jones wrinkled his slimy brow and snout and leaned toward Jack and Fitzwilliam. A tentacle slithered toward Jack, who recoiled in disgust. The tentacle reached out to Jack as if it were a finger, rested under his chin, and lifted his head threateningly toward the *Dutchman*'s captain, who towered above Jack.

"Listen here. I am in no mood for games, boy," Jones said. "Turn over the Timekeeper, or I will summon the Kraken."

"Bring on the beastie," Jack said bravely. "I've heard his terrible breath could kill a man, but it can't be much worse than yours, mate."

Davy Jones threateningly lifted up his staff.

"Do you want to know *how* I know you

know that I know you won't summon said beastie?" Jack asked. "Because if you do, down goes the wee *Barnacle*, down go Jack and Fitzy over here. And down goes this little timepiece everyone seems to have their knickers in a knot over."

"Fool," Davy Jones said. "I will enjoy tearing you apart with my bare hands."

"You call *those* hands?" Jack asked, eyeing Jones's claw and tentacle. "I guess it's all a matter of semantics. Anyway, I still don't know what you could ever want with this watch, Davy J, but if it's a fight you'd like . . ." Jack said, dangling the watch over the side of the *Barnacle*, coolly threatening to drop it.

Fitzwilliam and Jones yelled "No!" while simultaneously lunging for the watch, which Jack neatly pulled out of harm's way—harm in this case being the slimy, mad captain and the aristocratic know-it-all.

Turning, Fitzwilliam drew his sword and began to slash away at Jones, determined to be rid of the competition. Jones, however, managed to evade every one of the expert swordsman's swipes.

Jack casually hoisted himself up onto the side of the *Barnacle* and watched as the two rather odd opponents dueled . . . for a pocket watch. Jack smirked at the ridiculousness of the situation, and then the smirk suddenly vanished as he felt something whip around his neck. It was Davy Jones's tentacled arm, and it was quickly tightening its grip. Jack choked and gasped, attempting to speak, but he couldn't force out any air.

"Give. Me. The. Watch. Now," Jones said.

Jack was turning a pale shade of blue under Jones's tight grip. As Jack lifted up his hand, Jones grabbed the watch, angrily gripping the chain with one of the tentacles of his beard.

With no further use for Jack, Jones released him. Jack fell to the deck and gasped for air.

Fitzwilliam, who was not willing to lose his precious watch—his last memento of his departed sister—once again lunged at Jones. He quickly severed the tentacle that held the watch, causing Jones to wail in agony. The timepiece fell to the deck, landing near Jack, who reached out his hand and recovered it.

"I think you've made him quite angry, Fitzy," Jack wheezed, still having difficulty talking.

"What would ever make you think that?" Fitzwilliam asked Jack, eying Jones's slashed tentacle, which gushed with a bluish fluid.

"What is so bloody special about this rusty old thing, anyway?" Jack asked, clearly

frustrated that everyone seemed to know something about this watch that still eluded him.

Flipping the top of the timepiece open, Jack accidentally lifted the crown—the knob used to wind the watch and adjust the time— and instantly, the whole commotion aboard the *Barnacle* quieted. In fact, *everything*, for as far as Jack's eyes could see, was completely and utterly still.

CHAPTER TWO

Silence.

Jack Sparrow had not known the true meaning of the word until this very moment. The world around him was now completely motionless. Even the distant sounds that feebly make their way to ears during moments of quiet were absent. There was no rustling of wind, no squawking of seabirds, no quiet lapping of waves.

This threw Jack into a bit of a stupor. But, as with all the strange and amazing things he had experienced on his adventures, Jack adapted to the noiseless world rather quickly and relatively easily. Soon, he was skipping along the *Barnacle*'s deck, searching the sea for any indication of passing time.

Above Jack, the clouds were firmly fixed in the sky. The sea was stiller than glass, and in the distance Jack could see fish frozen in mid leap. Droplets of water, suspended in the air around the sea creatures, appeared to defy gravity. The sun was still. The air was still. Everything was still . . . except for Jack Sparrow.

"Oh, boy," Jack said.

Jack paced the deck, examining the watch. Obviously it was the timepiece that had caused this oddest of occurrences. No wonder Jones was so desperate to get his tentacled hand on it.

Jack toyed with the crown, considering whether he should reactivate time. Part of him wondered if he *could* even do so. What if the watch didn't work both ways? What if by pulling on the crown, he had halted everything around him forever? He'd be doomed to a world free of people, free of pirates and the Royal Navy and absentee fathers and runaway aristocrats.

A wide smile crept across Jack's face.

Maybe this wasn't so terrible after all.

Jack walked port side, then starboard. Then port again. Then starboard once more.

What would he do first?

He continued to pace. He saw a line of brown and green to the west. There was an island in the distance—and it wasn't that far off. He could grab the skiff that the crew kept belowdecks and row over to it. He had all the time in the world to get there. Maybe he'd find a town. Then he could "borrow" all of the gold and riches and spices that he found. Then again, what would they matter if there were no one else in the world? He seemed to realize that the value of gold—or anything for that matter—was relative. If no one was there to demand it, it suddenly became worthless.

"So gold and riches have no integrity all their own," Jack said, responding aloud to his own reverie. "Hmm. That's not very exciting. Takes all the fun out of it."

With the thrill of pillaging and plunder-ing gone, Jack turned to other things he might be able to do.

"Well, I have always wanted to see the great waterfalls of South America. But they won't be doing much 'falling' with time stopped and all that nonsense," Jack said, relinquishing his dream of cascading over the tallest of the waterfalls in a barrel.

In fact, everything he thought of, every option he had, seemed to be no fun without time moving things along.

Jack sighed. "I guess I'll need to turn my attention to this here ship of mine and the passengers aboard her. A captain's work is endless, is it not?"

Clasping his hands behind his back, Jack walked over to Fitzwilliam and Davy Jones, who both stood stone still. The two looked more like statues than living beings. Fitzwilliam was locked in position with his arm stretched toward Jack. His mouth was wide open, his hair completely stiff where it had been blowing in the sea air, his hand braced on his sword. He looked dignified and heroic, and if he *were* a statue, he'd perfectly commemorate some great battle.

Jack sized up his frozen crewmate. "The

part suits you. And best of all, you're not able to jabber on with that aristocratic, stuffity-stuff mouth of yours."

Enjoying the freedom to say and do whatever he liked, Jack now threw an arm over Fitzwilliam's shoulder and turned to Jones. While he was as immobile as Fitzwilliam, the captain of the *Flying Dutchman* was no less horrifying to look at in his current state than he had been when he was able to move about freely. His staff was planted firmly on the deck, and the tentacles of his beard were stiff and still. This, however, did not affect Jack enough to keep him quiet.

"Well, well, well," Jack said. "If it isn't the captain of the *Flying Dutchman* come aboard my ship—*uninvited* I might add!"

Jack turned to Fitzwilliam.

"What say we toss this fishy specimen overboard, Fitzy?" Jack said, knowing full-well his friend couldn't respond. Jack put his ear next to Fitzwilliam's open mouth, pretending to be conversing with his silent crewmate.

"What's that, Fitzy? Oh, yes, yes, you are very right. Wish I were as quick as you, Fitz. We would not want to incur the wrath of so vile a villain. So, what shall we do?"

Jack paused a moment, again pretending that Fitzwilliam was replying. Then he nodded vigorously at whatever it was his crewmate *wasn't* saying.

"Right you are, mate. We do need to get off this boat and away from squiggly-face over here. But how?" Jack tilted his head, as if he were still in conversation with his motionless friend.

"Oh, no, I couldn't do that. You could drown, mate. *Drown*, do you hear? What's that? Yes, yes, well, I guess you're right. A captain's got to do what a captain's got to do."

Jack held up his index finger. "But first," he said, "I need to make sure I will in fact be able to start ye ol' world right back up again at some point in the future, assuming that a future exists in a world void of time. So pardon me for a moment while I step to the other side of the boat, away from you two mates."

Striding over to the stern, Jack took a very deep breath and exhaled slowly. Then he looked down at the watch, flipped the lid, and pushed down the crown.

Jack was hit so hard by the sudden shift back to movement and sound that he stumbled backward and nearly toppled over.

Meanwhile, Fitzwilliam and Jones looked utterly nonplussed. Jones tossed his slimy head, searching for Jack, who had been standing before him a moment ago and was no longer there. Fitzwilliam was just as confused, and his eyes darted all over the *Barnacle* in search of Jack. Then, they both spotted him at the helm.

"How ever did you . . ." Fitzwilliam began.

Jones did not bother with questions. Instead, howling a beastly roar, he rushed Jack. When the captain of the *Dutchman* was just inches away from turning him into fish food, Jack casually lifted the crown from the watch once more.

And, again, everything stopped.

Jack smiled, satisfied.

"Now," he said, "best get to work."

CHAPTER THREE

With Jones and Fitzwilliam safely frozen once again, Jack stomped over to the trapdoor leading belowdecks. He descended the small stairway, ducking to clear the low overhead. Once down there, he lit a torch and surveyed the space. Since most of his crew had left him,* Jack had not done as good a job as he would have hoped in keeping the *Barnacle* shipshape and organized.

*In Vol. 7, *City of Gold*

"Now, where is that decaying mess of a skiff?" Jack asked, scanning the area. He lit a torch and waved it over the cluttered heaps of odds and ends piled everywhere. But like the *Barnacle*, the skiff was made of wood, and so wherever it was, it blended into the boat as well as a chameleon might.

Troves of jewels, gleaned from the *Barnacle*'s very first adventure, were tossed carelessly about the room. Rubies and diamonds sparkled, and gold chains and pieces of eight glittered under the torchlight. It was this treasure that had allowed them the freedom to continue on their adventures. The sale of just a handful of these precious items had kept the crew going for months at a time.

But the below-deck area was not cluttered with riches alone. Off in a far corner sat a pile of empty glass jars picked up in

Antigua, which Jack had insisted might come in handy someday. (Thus far, they had only proved to take up much-needed space.) In addition, there was more kindling tossed about than would be found at a witch's trial and certainly more than the crew would ever need. Piles of clothing, mostly belonging to Jack's former crewmates, were stacked along the walls.

"Should send those rags to Davy Jones's Locker," Jack said, a little bitterly. Then he let out a shout. "Aha!" He had spotted something large and wooden beneath a pile of things, including a taxidermic duck he'd picked up off the coast of Florida. Walking over to the object, he began to dust it off.

But the more Jack saw of the object, the more confused he became. He started swatting the dust off of it more furiously.

"What the devil is this?" he said, tossing

the stuffed duck and the other random items off the wooden object as he dragged it into fuller view. The large wooden mass wasn't the skiff he was expecting at all. In fact, it was something Jack had never seen before. But since it was here, aboard the *Barnacle*, it was something he *should* have seen, had he or any member of his crew put it there.

"What do we have here?" Jack asked, examining the large, carved slab of wood closely. It was just about the same size as the skiff, but instead of being hollowed out, it was round and the surface was adorned with numerous faces—what appeared to be representations of the heathen gods he had heard so much about since sailing the Seven Seas.

"A totem," Jack mused. "The last time I saw one of these I was off the coast of Rhode Island." Jack knew that only the people who had lived in the northeast colonies before the colonists arrived were known to carve such things. So how in blazes did it get here aboard the *Barnacle*? And more important, where was the bloody skiff?

Jack shrugged, deciding that he was not going to find the skiff in among the mess belowdecks. And, moreover, he realized he could do the job with the materials he had at hand. He braced the totem to his back using some spare lines and, whistling between groans of exertion, carried the pole up onto the deck. There, he untied the lines from his waist and the totem thumped onto the planked floor. Jack jumped, startled, as even the slightest noise could rattle someone's nerves in an otherwise silent world, no less a thundering crash.

It took Jack a moment to remember that his "crewmates"—Fitzwilliam and Jones—

would not be reacting to the crash. He could handle this situation any way he liked. Neither Fitzwilliam nor Jones was aware of his own current state. Jack had proven this earlier, when he started time and they were confused by Jack's "disappearance." Whatever was happening on the deck was not registering with these two—which was incredibly advantageous to him at this particular juncture in his scheming.

Still smiling, Jack rolled the totem between his last remaining crewmate and the towering, slithering captain who had so rudely boarded Jack's vessel.

"Sorry 'bout this mate," Jack said to Jones. "This ship's not big enough for all of us."

Jack stood back, taking in this bizarre sight one last time. Then he got to work. Turning, he poked Fitzwilliam, attempting to tip him over the way one might topple a sleeping cow. When Fitzwilliam didn't budge, Jack attempted it again, this time with more force. Still nothing. Growing aggravated, Jack ran toward the aristocrat with full force, and upon impact, the still body of his crewmate crashed to the deck— with Jack on top of him! Jack quickly jumped up and dusted himself off, as if he didn't want to be contaminated with whatever it was that made Fitzwilliam so annoying.

Looking down, Jack considered his fallen mate, then the totem, then the slack line that he had used to carry the pole up on deck. His plan was proving more difficult than expected. Sighing, he rolled Fitzwilliam on top of the totem, then he fastened him to it using the lines.

"This had better work," Jack grunted. Then he added, "Although if it doesn't, I'll never have to hear your pompous voice again!"

Using all of his might, Jack hauled the totem—along with Fitzwilliam, who was tied to it—over to the side of the ship. He was having a bit of trouble, so he turned to Jones.

"Excuse me, sir, mind if I borrow your stick?" Jack asked, peeling Jones's tentacled hand off his staff and taking it from him. "Thank you kindly."

Using the staff for leverage, Jack was able to hoist the totem up against the side of the ship. The totem teetered on the *Barnacle*'s railing, as if it were balanced on a fulcrum.

"Well, here goes nothing," Jack said, closing his eyes and pushing the totem—and Fitzwilliam with it—off the side of the *Barnacle*. Jack rushed to the railing to watch it crash into the sea. His eyes grew wide.

The bobbing wood floated alongside the boat. Jack had anticipated that Fitzwilliam would have ended up floating on *top* of the totem. Instead, the aristocrat was now sub-merged *under* the water, with only his hands and feet visible from beneath the totem. It looked as if a tree had fallen on top of him. The shock of his crewmate's submersion quickly faded, and Jack couldn't help but laugh a little bit. He realized that with all time stopped, Fitzwilliam was not breathing. So, Jack decided, he could probably stay sub-merged as long as Jack kept time under his thumb.

Jack turned to Davy Jones and gave a little bow.

"Nice seeing you, gent. It was wonderful to have the pleasure of catching up," Jack said. "You certainly don't disappoint. Ta for now!"

Then he leaped over the rail, hopped on top of the floating totem pole, and began to paddle leisurely for the shore—leaving Jones and the *Barnacle* behind.

CHAPTER FOUR

*A*fter some time—and in truth, it was only "some time" to *Jack*; for the rest of the world no time had passed *at all*—Jack reached the shore. He dragged the totem pole out of the water, and Fitzwilliam with it. Having been submerged the whole time, the nobleman's son was soaked—not to mention rather pruny—adding weight to the pole and making it very difficult to pull him from the water. Once Jack had finally done so, he untied the boy and dragged him further up onto the shore of the island at which they'd arrived.

Propping Fitzwilliam against the totem, Jack hit the aristocrat's back a few times, just to make sure he had not swallowed any water on their voyage over to the island. Then he sat down next to the other boy and took out the pocket watch.

"Do I really want to do this to myself?" Jack asked, a pensive expression crossing his face. Then he slumped down, put his hand on the watch's crown and pushed it down, starting up the watch. The great rush of sound and movement hit Jack once more, startling him anew. He quickly stopped the watch again and attempted to catch his breath from the fright. It would do no good for him to appear upset upon "waking" the stuffy aristocrat.

When his breathing had returned to

normal, Jack cleared his throat and thrust out his chest proudly, as though he had never been frightened in the first place. Then he straightened his back and pushed the crown of the timepiece down once more. The rush of sound and shadow came again, but this time Jack was prepared. He smoothly pocketed the watch, hiding it just as Fitzwilliam burst to life.

"En garde!" the aristocrat shouted, leaping forward, his hand on his sword.

"Calm down, mate," Jack said.

"What in the name of—? Where am I?" Fitzwilliam asked. "What has happened? Jack, the last I saw you, you were—*we* were—where is the *Barnacle*? Where is Jones?"

"I don't know from this *Barnacle* and Jones you speak of," Jack said, feigning ignorance.

"Do not toy with me, Jack," Fitzwilliam said.

"Oh, but it's such fun," Jack responded.

Fitzwilliam held his sword to Jack's throat. He looked very threatening, with his wet hair dripping down in front of his livid eyes. Jack threw up his hands in resignation.

"You see, Fitzy," Jack said, backing away, "I saved you from the tentacled clutches of the nasty Jones *and* tried to keep him from gaining hold of your precious timepiece. Speaking of which, that there watch of yours seems to make time go all funny. Stops it, in fact. Has it always done so?"

"I have no idea what you are talking about. You are a madman and speak non-sense," Fitzwilliam replied. "Time does not stop. Ever."

"Fitzy, Fitzy, Fitzy, no need to resort to name calling. Now with you the owner of a watch with such interesting properties, it begs the question—what other secrets are you keeping from me? Are you a spy for the Royal Navy? A privateer of the East India Trading Company?" Jack asked.

Fitzwilliam opened his mouth to reply, but before he could finish, a furious voice rang out over the sea.

"Jack Sparrow!"

It was the unmistakable voice of Davy Jones. The *Dutchman* was just offshore and on board, Jones was clearly *very* angry.

"Oh, brilliant, Jack. There you go again, upsetting the immortals. Really wonderful," Fitzwilliam said, throwing up his arms in frustration.

"It didn't seem that you were willing to appease him by forfeiting that there watch of yours, mate. I did you a favor, attempting to help you keep it from him," Jack said.

"Well, then, I kindly ask you to *stop* doing me favors, '*Captain*'," Fitzwilliam said bitterly.

"You won't hear me arguing that," Jack said, dusting the sand off his pants.

"Fools! This is not the last you will hear of me," Jones's voice rang out again, interrupting the squabbling duo. Then, as the boys watched, off in the distance, the *Flying Dutchman* dipped below the waves and was gone.

"As angry as I am at you right now," Fitzwilliam said, "I cannot help but ask, as you appear to be the only other living soul in the vicinity, why he did not just come ashore and massacre us."

Jack sneered and lifted his nose in the air to indicate that he was not speaking to Fitzwilliam.

"Fine, Jack. Be like that," Fitzwilliam said. "At least he does not have my watch."

Jack cocked an eyebrow. "Oh," Jack said, thinking fast. "Oh, I forgot to tell you that

bit. Yes, yes, he does in fact have your watch. He grabbed it back from me before we left the ship. You just don't remember any of it because I pressed the watch, and time went all funny directly afterward and you must have forgotten." Jack made a face that looked more like he was trying to convince himself of this lie than Fitzwilliam.

"WHAT?" Fitzwilliam railed, surprising Jack by believing the tale. "All this: this journey to an island while I was somehow *unconscious*, this angering of Davy Jones, this endless danger you have put us both in . . . and *he* has what we were trying to *keep* from him anyway?"

"That's right," Jack said. "Live with it."

"I do not want to 'live with it,' and I no longer wish to deal with you, 'Captain' Sparrow. I am foolhardy for not joining the rest of the *Barnacle*'s crew as they escaped your far-from-expert command by joining the crew of the *Fleur de la Mort.*"

"Oh, Fitzy. That hurts," Jack said, making a pained expression and holding his hand to his heart. "That hurts me right here."

"Had you a heart, perhaps it would. But we all know better. However, would that I *could* truly hurt you, you had best believe I would. But we appear to be the only two men on this island, and we will need to assist one another if we are to escape from it alive. That is an unfortunate, but very real, truth," Fitzwilliam said.

Jack shook his head. "Oh, Fitzy, always so practical. Now, as I am clearly the brains of this outfit, as well as the saner of the two of us, what say we search for some fresh water, which must be in abundance on an island such as this, with it's thick and viny foliage."

"And why should we not just travel

back to the *Barnacle*? It is moored not far offshore," Fitzwilliam said.

"Um, I don't think you want to do that, mate."

"Why ever not?"

"Legend has it that Jones can step on land but once every ten years. You're safer here on this island, at least for the time being," Jack said.

"And if this is the stuff of 'legend,' why should I believe such rubbish?"

"Fine, Fitzy, take your chances, then," Jack said, walking away. "Just don't come crying after me when Jones's grand old beastie is wrapping its tentacles around your ankles and pulling you down to a watery grave."

Fitzwilliam blanched at the thought of the Kraken attacking him. Then he sped up to fall in step with Jack, who had already advanced ten yards ahead of the aristocrat.

"You know that I hate you," Fitzwilliam said.

"I wouldn't have it any other way," Jack responded.

CHAPTER FIVE

"We have been walking for hours, Jack. And this jungle only grows denser as we walk on," Fitzwilliam said. He paused to wipe the sweat from his brow. "I am not convinced that you could find a way out of these thick environs even if you were promised the gift of immortality were you to accomplish the task," Fitzwilliam continued. "Not only that, but we have yet to find potable water and we are sopping wet. And in this humidity, nothing on our persons has had the opportunity or the means to dry."

Ignoring Fitzwilliam's complaining, Jack walked on, choping away at the vines and shrubbery that covered the island.

"*And*," Fitzwilliam went on, "we have heaven-knows-what-kind of insects buzzing about our ears, parasites leeching on our skin, and lion-sized mosquitoes sucking our veins dry."

Jack swatted his forehead, squishing a particularly large bug. It made a crunching sound as its oozy, bluish white guts smeared all over Jack's face and hand.

"Eww," Jack said, holding his hand out to examine the crushed insect, whose legs twitched in the final throes of death.

"And besides that," Fitzwilliam finished, "we have not eaten a right meal in days."

Jack offered the dying bug in his hand to

Fitzwilliam. The aristocrat sneered. Jack shrugged and popped the beetlelike insect into his own mouth.

"Don't complain to me about not eating if you're going to be picky, mate," Jack said with a full mouth.

"You disgust me," Fitzwilliam said, wrinkling his nose.

"And you disgust me," Jack retorted, stopping in a clearing. "So what say we just shake hands here and now, say *sayonara* and go our separate ways."

"You know full-well we cannot do that, Jack," Fitzwilliam said.

"Watch me," Jack replied, before saluting Fitzwilliam and marching away.

"Jack . . ." Fitzwilliam said.

Without turning around, Jack waved bye-bye over his shoulder and continued to stroll away with pomp, his hips swaying dramatically. Then, without warning, the ground collapsed beneath him.

"Aaaaah!" Jack screamed.

"Jack!" Fitzwilliam cried, running over to the place where he had fallen.

"Down here, down here," Jack called out, frustrated.

He had fallen into a hole that was about six feet wide and twice his height. Thankfully he had not been killed, or even badly hurt, but the hole was certainly deep enough that he could not easily escape.

"Just give me a moment," Fitzwilliam said desperately, suddenly beginning to imagine a future stranded on this desert island all alone. Jack might be annoying, but Fitzwilliam had learned over time that he also had a gift for getting out of trouble—a gift that Fitzwilliam could not rightly claim for himself.

"Aaaaaah!" Jack screamed again.

"What is it now, Jack?" Fitzwilliam said, "I told you I am in the process of figuring—"

"Aaaaah! Aaaaah! Aaaaah!" Jack squealed.

Fitzwilliam rushed over to the pit and peered into it.

"What is wrong?"

"Besides me being stuck in a hole, mate?" Jack asked sarcastically. "I seem to have some friends down here with me."

Jack lifted up a handful of wriggling bugs—similar to the cockroachlike one he'd recently swatted on his forehead. They were of many different shapes and sizes.

"Oh, my . . ." Fitzwilliam said, stepping backward in disgust. Then, suddenly, the ground fell out from under the aristocrat's feet, too.

"Jack," a voice came from the hole that Fitzwilliam had tumbled into.

"What?" Jack's voice came, flatly, from the other hole.

If at that moment an unwitting person had happened to walk past, it would seem as if two gaping holes were talking to one another.

"I have fallen into a hole of similar size to the one in which you currently find yourself."

"I discerned as much," Jack said from his hole.

"Well?"

"Well? What do you mean 'well'?"

"What are we going to do?"

"You tell me, Fitzy. *You* were the one who was free to roam about up there, and instead of doing everything in your power to remove me from this awful roach pit, you went and tumbled into *another* one. Not, mind you, that you hadn't been forewarned by the terrible event that had befallen me—oh, just *moments* before. Bravo."

"Well . . ."

"There you go with your 'wells' again. *Nothing* is well right now, nothing at all."

"If you would have let me *finish*, Sparrow," Fitzwilliam's voice came booming from his hole, "I was attempting to say that perhaps there is some way to scale the walls of our respective pits."

Inside his hole, Jack rolled his eyes, and Fitzwilliam, inside his own, imagined Jack doing just that. The boy who fancied himself a captain might have been ingenious when it came to escape plans, but he and his reactions were fairly predictable.

"Oh, Fitzy!" Jack said in a tone that oozed mock admiration. "Why did I not think of that clever plan myself? Maybe because—*it won't work.*"

"It was just a thought," Fitzwilliam said.

"Well, you should stop thinking," Jack replied. "It seems to do nothing but get us both into trouble."

Despite Jack's prediction, Fitzwilliam attempted to grapple the walls of his hole and began to scale up the side. He did not meet with much success, and he yelped as the soft walls crumbled around him.

"You *had* to go and try it anyway, didn't you?" Jack said from his hole, recognizing the telltale sound of crumbling dirt and loose stones coming from Fitz's ditch. "Keep climbing, mate. Soon you'll be buried neck-high in collapsed mud and sand, and then I'll never have to see nor hear from you again."

"Do you have any better suggestions, 'Captain'?" Fitzwilliam shouted.

"As a matter of fact, I *do*," Jack shouted back.

"Do you mind sharing them?"

"I said I *have* them. I just have not had very much time to think them up yet. I am doing that now," Jack said.

"I thought you said thinking only landed a person in trouble," Fitzwilliam replied.

"I did not say 'a person,' I said 'you.' For, just as it is dangerous for those without feet to attempt to run, it is catastrophic for those without a brain to attempt to think. I, on the other hand—"

"*You* are mad, Jack. Insane. Complete institutional fodder," Fitzwilliam fumed. The aristocrat slumped in the pit, defeated, but immediately sprang back up again. He had sat down on something long and slithering—Jack may have been bothered by bugs, but Fitzwilliam now found himself faced with snakes!

"Ugh! Even Madame Minuit's slithering

reptiles were not so vile,"* Fitzwilliam said.

"Um, Fitzy," Jack called out from his ditch.

"What is it now?" Fitzwilliam asked.

"I don't think we're going to have to worry about getting ourselves out of here after all," Jack said with a clear mix of enthusiasm and trepidation.

"And why is that?" Fitzwilliam asked.

"Because," Jack said, "I think we're about to be rescued or taken captive . . . one or the other."

Fitzwilliam looked up, puzzled, as moving shadows were cast on the walls at the top of his hole. Then a group of men leaned down and peered into the hole, blocking out most of the sun. They held spears, and their

*Madame Minuit is the villainess who attacked Jack and the crew in Vol. 5, *The Age of Bronze*, and Vol. 7, *City of Gold*

elaborate palm-leaf headdresses ruffled in the humid breeze.

They shouted something in a language Fitzwilliam did not understand. But then, to his immense surprise, he heard Jack respond to them in whatever tongue they spoke.

"Hang on, Fitzy," Jack said when he had finished. "We're about to get out of here. That said, I'm not entirely certain if we'll be alive or dead next time we see each other."

CHAPTER SIX

A short while later, Jack and Fitzwilliam were being carried through the jungle by a dozen or so tall, angry warriors. As Jack had promised, the men had gotten them out of the holes. They had dropped crude ladders down to the boys, but then once they were out, the warriors hit them over the head and knocked them out. That was the last thing Jack and Fitzwilliam remembered. But sometime between that moment and the present one, they had been tied to two long poles. And now they were being transported somewhere.

The boys awoke at around the same time with screaming headaches. Jack glared at Fitzwilliam, who was opening his mouth to say something.

"Don't say it," Jack said.

"Don't say what?" Fitzwilliam asked.

"Don't say whatever you were going to say—surely some wise, smart little comment from your precious little mouth."

"I was just going to suggest that you speak their language—I heard you back when we were trapped in those holes—so why do you not try some of your famous diplomacy," Fitzwilliam said.

"I do not speak their language," Jack said, frustrated.

"Then what was it you were saying to

them prior to being lifted from the holes?" Fitzwilliam asked.

"Blasted if I know," Jack said. "I was simply throwing together all the various foreign words and phrases I've picked up over the years. Figured they'd probably understand one or two of them."

"Well, did they?" Fitzwilliam asked.

Jack cringed a little. "I think I might have offended them. First in Swedish, then in Cantonese, and finally in Bantu."

Frustrated with Jack, Fitzwilliam turned to the warriors. Upon closer inspection, Fitzwilliam's brow furrowed. They were certainly odd-looking warriors. While they were dressed in tribal garb, they all appeared very European. Jack and Fitzwilliam had not noticed this before, having been conked on the head the minute after they were rescued.

"Where are you taking us?" Fitzwilliam

asked, hopeful they'd be able to answer, given their European features. When his question met with no reply, he asked again, this time a little bit louder.

"You can quiet down, mate. They're not deaf, clearly they're just ignoring you," Jack said.

As if to emphasize the point, at that moment the warriors unceremoniously dropped the large poles that held Jack and Fitzwilliam. The boys yelped as they landed on their backs, still tied to their poles, in a muddy clearing. Jack craned his neck as best he could and looked around. They were in a small village of twelve huts arranged in a circle. In the center was a large pile of stones that housed a blazing fire.

"As if we *needed* more heat," Jack said, sweating heavily from the tropical weather.

"This is no mere flame," an unfamiliar voice responded.

Jack felt his bonds being loosened as he and Fitzwilliam were freed from the poles and dragged to their feet. In moments, each boy had four warriors flanking him, pointing their spears at his neck. Standing in front of Jack was an exceptionally tall man whose voice they had just heard. He was pale like the others, and his features were also European—a sharp nose, a square jaw, and fair hair.

"This is Chantico," the tall man said, motioning to the fire.

"I love Chantico!" Jack said enthusiastically. "Unless it's fried too long in dirty oil. Then it's just far too crispy, and my ulcer can't take much of it. . . ."

"Silence!" the towering warrior commanded.

Jack's mouth snapped shut.

"Chantico is the patron goddess of our

people. She has been worshipped here since man first laid claim to this island centuries ago. Through hurricane winds and floods—her fire has never been extinguished."

"Well, why don't you and your old flame over here just have a grand old time together? My crewmate and I will then shuffle along, and we can pretend we've never met. Savvy?" Jack asked.

"Jack, perhaps it would be better to curb your witty banter right now," Fitzwilliam hissed.

"Sorry," Jack said, "can't help it."

"Sirs," Fitzwilliam said, "we are glad to hear you speak our language. We mean you no harm. We have come here in search of nothing but water, and perhaps some sustenance. We will happily be on our way."

"You do not understand," the tall man said. "Since the time when this flame was first kindled, our Aztec brothers have been required to sustain her."

"'Aztec brothers'?" Jack said quietly to Fitzwilliam, skeptically examining the pale man from head to toe. "If he has Aztec brothers, I have a mermaid for a sister."

"We must feed Chantico, so that she may survive," the tall warrior finished.

"So, what's the problem, mate?" Jack asked. "There's coconuts aplenty here on this island. Or throw the fiery lass some chicken, why don't you? Thought I smelled some cooking on the way over here."

"That was not chicken," the man said.

Jack gulped.

"So are you saying that *we* are to be fed to *this* flame?" Fitzwilliam asked.

"Oh, no, no, no," the tall man responded. "You see, Chantico is the goddess of the family hearth. We are family, this is our hearth—*she* is our hearth. We would not dare feed her here."

Jack looked at Fitzwilliam and traced circles around his temple with his finger to indicate insanity.

Fitzwilliam kicked Jack.

"But, you see," the tall man continued, "she is also the goddess of volcanoes. . . ."

"Yes, yes," Jack said, rolling his eyes, "and of little lost girls and lonesome wives, too, I'm sure. What is your point?"

The tall man cackled. "You're a fool, little man," the warrior said.

Jack straightened his back. "I am not little. Though I do appreciate that you recognized that I am a man."

"We do not feed Chantico *here*," the man went on, gesturing to the lapping flames in the center of the small village.

"Oh, thank goodness," Fitzwilliam said.

"We feed her—*there!*" The man pointed up to the top of a mountain peak, which until that moment, Jack and Fitzwilliam had failed to notice.

Now, the last two remaining crew members of the *Barnacle* squinted their eyes and looked up. There was a lot of mist at the top of this particular mountain, excessive even for a steamy jungle island like this one.

Then, without warning, a huge, explosive sound rang out, and the earth beneath them shook. The houses of the village rumbled, and Jack, Fitzwilliam, and even some of the warriors lost their balance. Then, from the very top of the mountain, rock and ash shot everywhere, and a huge plume of smoke spewed forth. A monstrous belching sound rang out over the entire island.

"Chantico is hungry," the tall warrior said. Then his eyes sparkled as he grinned devilishly.

CHAPTER SEVEN

$\mathcal{J}$ack and Fitzwilliam knew where this situation was headed—and it was nowhere good.

"Listen, mate," Jack said to the decked-out warrior who'd been addressing them. "Not sure what you're looking for exactly— though a new getup might be a good place to start—" Jack's voice fell to a whisper as he nodded toward Fitzwilliam. Leaning closer to the warrior chief, he continued, "My lordship over there is worth a pretty sixpence piece, if you know what I am alluding to. . . ."

The warrior's brow furrowed, and he eyed Jack in confusion.

Jack raised his eyebrows and frantically tossed his head in Fitzwilliam's direction. "Money, *dinero*, dubloons, et cetera . . ."

Jack was getting frustrated at the warrior's lack of understanding about where he was going with this. He decided to spell it out for him.

"We take the rich fop, put him up for ransom, and split our earnings, savvy?" he finally shouted. "You get some new clothes, some new food for Chantico. I get a new ship and crew, maybe?"

Fitzwilliam's face went red with fury and indignation.

The warrior seemed just as unhappy with the offer. He spit in Jack's face and shouted

something to the villagers, clearly com-
manding them to take Jack and Fitzwilliam
away.

"No hard feelings," Jack said to
Fitzwilliam as a blindfold was placed over
his eyes and the sunlight disappeared.

"I am not speaking to you," Fitzwilliam
said with a self-assured steadfastness.

A moment later, Fitzwilliam, too, was
blindfolded. And without further adieu, the
warriors dragged them away . . . toward the
very hungry Chantico.

A silent hour or so later, the warriors finally
stopped their marching. While their eyes
were still covered, Jack and Fitzwilliam
could smell the sulfuric odor issuing from
the cone of the volcano. Judging from the
intense smell and overwhelming heat, it was
clear they were *very* close.

Suddenly, Jack's blindfold was pulled off. Looking around, he saw that they were now in the middle of a molten alcove. Fitzwilliam's cloth had been removed as well, and when their eyes met, Fitzwilliam shot Jack a look that was almost as searing as the lava nearby.

Turning, Jack addressed their captors: "I don't know who you gents think you're fooling," Jack shouted, his voice echoing in the hollow of the cave. "I've never met an Aztec quite as pale as any of you, nor has any member of the Aztec nation ever attempted to feed me to a hungry volcano-god, though, I posit, if they had I wouldn't be here having this conversation with you, in which case my entire point is somewhat moot."

One of the warriors shoved Jack forward. Jack's hands and feet were still bound, and he hopped a few times trying to maintain his balance, but eventually toppled to the hard, volcanic floor of the cave. Squirming, he turned himself over, and just as he was about to prop himself up and open his mouth to utter another word of protest, *wham!*, Fitzwilliam came crashing down on top of him.

"Mrind mrgretting mroff mrof mmre?" Jack muttered, his voice muffled under Fitzwilliam's weight.

The aristocrat muscled his way off Jack. "You will pay for this," Fitzwilliam said angrily. "The entire Royal Navy will be looking for me."

"Yeah!" Jack said.

"I was talking to you, buffoon."

"'Buffoon'?" Jack said, mocking Fitzwilliam's choice of insults. "And, hey, I thought you weren't talking to me," he added.

"Oh, shut up," Fitzwilliam said.

While some of the warriors had been busy depositing Jack and Fitzwilliam in the cave, a second group had been sealing up the small entrance with large clusters of volcanic rock. Only the top remained to be filled, and as the two boys watched, the final warriors that were left in the cave climbed out of the opening.

"Hey, mates," Jack shouted, "mind leaving just that top portion open for some light and ventilation, like a window of sorts?"

At that moment, the final rocks were placed in the opening, and Jack and Fitzwilliam were left lying on the floor of the cave, the only light coming from two flickering torches and the few shafts of sunlight that had managed to make their way through the rocks sealing the entrance. The two had landed face-to-face and looked at each other bitterly as silence filled the room.

"Why could they not have just thrown us into the volcano and gotten it over with quickly, just as they do in all of the old tales?" Fitzwilliam finally asked, speaking more to himself than to Jack—but that didn't prevent Jack from answering.

"Volcano fumes are poisonous, Fitzy," Jack said smugly.

"So the whole of them would have died with us had they dropped us in the cone," Fitzwilliam mused. "Better to leave us here—let the lava flow over the opening they've blocked up."

"Exactly," Jack replied, almost as if he admired the thinking behind the plan.

"Seal the entrance. Seal our fates," Fitzwilliam muttered.

Jack rolled his eyes. "Even in the hour of your death, you are a dramatist, my liege."

"Hardly dramatic, 'Captain.' Is this is a

fine end for one to meet, in your opinion?" Fitzwilliam asked. "Especially one such as *me*? I flee from my overbearing father, leave behind a life of privilege, come face-to-face with the undead—on more than one occasion—battle vicious pirates, mermaids, storm kings, and snake women, only to perish tied up in a dark cave with the last person on earth I would wish to perish with."

"Sounds as though you are living quite vicariously through me," Jack said flatly. "After all, *I* was the one who battled the mermaids, the storm king, and the snake woman. So I would say your assessments are quite inaccurate. As such, you should be *honored* to perish with me."

"Oh, who do you think you are fooling, Jack? You—you, who has deluded yourself into believing you have a *ship*, that you are a *captain*."

"Well, I don't think any of that matters much anymore now, eh?" Jack pointed out.

"Oh, it does, Jack Sparrow. It will matter till you and I take our last breaths in this heaven-forsaken death cave here."

"No, it *really* doesn't matter," Jack continued, "not with that big beastie about to tear into us."

"Now what are you on about?" Fitzwilliam asked.

There was a loud rumble in the cave.

"*That* beastie is what I am talking about," Jack answered.

"That rumbling was nothing more than the volcano that will be killing us a short time from now," Fitzwilliam said.

"No. That was the rumbling tummy of a big, hungry kitty with very sharp teeth who will be dining on us sooner than said volcano and its patron, Chantico, will be."

"What are you on about, Jack?" Fitz-william said, flipping himself over so that he and Jack were facing in the same direction.

And that's when he saw it—a huge, vicious, hungry jaguar. The cat's eyes were flickering menacingly with the reflection of the burning torches. His powerful jaw was stretched open, and his fangs were bared. Then he let out the loudest growl that Jack and Fitzwilliam had ever heard, or more accurately, the loudest growl since they'd last seen Davy Jones.

"We are like cake on a platter to this beast," Fitzwilliam said, more calmly than one might expect for someone who was about to be devoured by a jaguar.

Jack, on the other hand, was squirming like mad.

"You will never make your way out of those bonds. You will do nothing but entice the beast, Jack," Fitzwilliam said. "Unless, of course, that is your aim—to hasten your demise."

"Will you shut your gangplank for one moment?" Jack shouted. Fitzwilliam could not see for the darkness and the angle, but Jack was struggling to reach something. And it felt like he almost had it.

"I just do not see what the use is, I mean—" Fitzwilliam began.

But in that moment, the jaguar growled louder than ever, squatted on its haunches—then pounced toward the two helpless boys.

And then something happened.

Or, more accurately, nothing happened.

The beast was frozen in midair. Fitzwilliam had stopped rambling.

Only Jack was moving.

Despite the fact that his hands were still bound, he had managed to reach the watch, lift the crown, and buy himself some time. In fact, he now had all the time he could possibly need.

Thinking quickly, Jack squirmed over to the wall of the cave and propped himself up. When he was finally standing, he hopped over to where the jaguar was suspended in midair. Maneuvering his hands, Jack leaned in toward the violent beast and gazed into its deadly maw. Even though Jack knew the jaguar was powerless at this moment, he couldn't stop a shiver of fear as he stared into its mouth, which was full of rows of saberlike fangs and reeked of previous fleshy meals.

Once Jack had shaken off the creeps, he leaned in and went to work, sawing away his bonds on the jaguar's teeth. Very quickly—a testament to the sharpness of the cat's teeth—his hands were free. He went to work

loosening the ties on his legs and then reopened the passageway into the cave that the warriors had sealed off. It seemed that the warriors had all gone. Which, Jack had to admit, was rather smart, as a thick plume of smoke hung overhead and the volcano appeared ready to erupt.

But Jack didn't have to worry about that. Every moment was his. After all, he was controlling time.

Jack smiled, dusted himself off, and then grabbed a torch of still flame to better see inside the cave. After taking a closer look at the frozen jaguar, he made his way out of the cave.

Then he remembered something.

"I should really take him with me," he said, sounding more than just a little bit inconvenienced.

CHAPTER EIGHT

$\mathcal{B}$y the time Jack managed to untie Fitzwilliam and drag him out of the cave, he was completely exhausted. Then Jack peered down the incredibly steep slope of the volcano mount and groaned.

"This is *not* going to work," he said flatly.

Jack looked at Fitzwilliam. Then he peered down the slope again. Then he glanced back at the cave that contained a very angry, hungry, and possibly rabid jaguar. Of course, the jaguar was currently frozen in time, like Fitzwilliam and every-thing else in existence, save Jack himself. But even with all the time in the world at his disposal, Jack knew he would not be able to safely lower himself and Fitzwilliam to the bottom of the steep slope. Then he thought of something.

"How did they march us up here? After all, there has to be a way down if there was a way up. If not for those blasted blindfolds this would be so much easier."

Having no other choice, if he didn't want to take a tumble down the slope, Jack inched along the perimeter of the tiny cliff that presided over the unimaginably steep drop. When he got to the very edge, he noticed something . . . a walkway, constructed of rope and metal, bridging a chasm.

"Aha!" Jack shouted gleefully. Then he cautiously hurried back to Fitzwilliam, grabbed him under the arms, and began to drag him across the bridge. The aristocrat's polished buckle shoes (Jack could never understand how he managed to spar so well in them, or how he managed to keep them immaculate) clanked like a piece of metal stuck in a wheel spoke as Jack dragged him along.

By the time he had gotten almost all the way across the feeble bridge, Jack was too tired to be the least bit happy that he was escaping.

With a groan of exhaustion, he put his foot down and stepped right on . . . nothing at all! For a moment, Jack—and Fitzwilliam with him—swayed precariously. When Jack finally managed to steady them, he looked down and noticed a huge hole in the bridge, which revealed a long drop into . . . nothing. The warriors had taken the precaution of destroying the bridge as they left. The wooden planks on the last twenty feet had been shattered!

"Blast it all!" Jack shouted.

He looked back at the hundred yards or so that he had managed to drag his crewmate across. He was *not* going to do that all over again.

"Only one thing that can be done," Jack said.

He took out the watch once more and pushed the crown down, starting the clock—and time—once more.

"What—where? Jack, what have you done to me now?" Fitzwilliam asked.

Jack quickly hid the watch, knowing Fitzwilliam would want it back.

"Me? Oh, nothing, nothing at all mate. It's this odd island. Seems to just—" Jack waved his hand airily, "pick us up and deposit us wherever it wishes with no memory of how it happened. At least we are free of that hungry cat, no?" Jack's eyes grew wide with a look that could either mean he was mad with brilliance, or just plain mad.

"You are mad! Mad, mad, *mad!*" Fitzwilliam shouted, obviously not concerned about what particular kind of madness was afflicting Jack. "Islands do not just choose to move people around. And in the event that they could decide to do so, they would not have the means to accomplish such a task as they are *inanimate!*"

"Right, mate. And next you're going to tell me there's no such thing as Davy Jones, or Tia Dalma . . . or Father Christmas," Jack said evenly.

He had a point. After all the crew had experienced, was it really so unreasonable to believe that an island could have a mind of its own? Or the ability to carry out its wishes?

Their discussion was cut short by an

exceptionally loud rumble. Jack jumped and let out a little squeal when he heard it, automatically thinking it must be the jaguar they'd left behind, anxious to reclaim its meal. It was only after Jack took a whiff of the awful-smelling air that he realized it was much worse than that.

"Oh, wonderful," Jack said.

Fitzwilliam could not speak. His mouth hung open as he looked up toward the peak of the volcano, which had begun to spew large rocks from its mouth.

"Careful there, mate," Jack said, grabbing Fitzwilliam by the arm and pulling him from the path of an exceptionally large semimolten rock as it plummeted to earth, barely missing the two boys and the bridge.

"What do you suggest we do now?" Fitzwilliam asked, with more than a hint of sarcasm in his voice.

"What we always do . . ." Jack responded.

"Run?"

"Right you are, mate," Jack answered.

As the two boys retraced their steps on the bridge, the volcano blew its top over their heads. Jack screamed and covered his head to protect himself.

"It is no use! We are doomed!" Fitzwilliam shouted.

Just then, a river of lava began spilling down the mountainside.

"Whether you believe it or not, I am not going to argue with you," Jack said.

The molten river was taking down everything in its path—rocks, soil, trees. . . .

"Trees!" Jack shouted suddenly.

"What?" Fitzwilliam asked.

"Just follow my lead," Jack said, "and don't jump too soon—or too late."

As the stream of lava rushed closer and

closer, Jack readied himself by squatting, as if he were a cat prepared to pounce on his prey. Then, just before the boiling liquid rock had reached them, Jack yelled, "NOW!" and the two boys leaped into the top of a particularly full, uprooted tree that was caught in the lava flow, and began to ride it down the unbelievably steep slope of the mountain.

"This is lunacy," Fitzwilliam yelled over the roaring rush of lava.

"Got any better ideas?" Jack asked.

"The tree is burning, Jack!" Fitzwilliam yelled.

He was right. The flames were quickly engulfing the trunk, and in moments, the two boys were surrounded by fire.

"Look!" Jack shouted.

They were passing by another tree the lava flow was about to fell. Fitzwilliam nodded vigorously, and the two boys jumped onto the new tree. As the lava carried them down the mountain, they watched their previous tree disintegrate into ash. The boys continued their tree-jumping. Then, suddenly, out of the corner of his eye, Jack saw a glint in the sunlight. As he jumped onto yet another tree, he saw what was causing the glinting—it was a lake! And it looked to be in the path of the lava. If they could make their way over, they would have a safe way out of this exceedingly hot situation.

"Fitz! Bear right!" Jack ordered.

Confused at first, Fitzwilliam understood what Jack was doing when he looked over and saw the lake. Without a word, the two began to leap from tree to tree, moving closer and closer to the lake. And then, just as they had leaped onto the last possible tree, the lava poured into the cold lake, quickly coagulating. They had made it.

As they waded in the lake, they could feel it growing increasingly hotter from the lava flow. Both of them were coughing from the smoke they'd inhaled and the stench of burning soil and melting rock as they tried to swim to a safer shore. Then, Jack noticed something else.

"Over there!" Jack shouted, pointing to a huge Aztec-style building that was on higher ground.

"Judging from how well we were received the first time we encountered people on this island, I sincerely doubt we will find anyone friendly in that place," Fitzwilliam warned.

"Friendly? Perhaps not. But it *will* provide shelter," Jack said, "at least until this whole volcano hoopla has blown over."

Fitzwilliam shrugged, clearly beyond the point of caring. He and Jack rushed to the grand entrance of what looked like an Aztec temple. But while most Aztec temples had fallen into ruin since the age of the conquistadors, this one looked almost pristine. Jack opened the huge doors, and the two boys entered.

"Looks empty enough," Jack said, his eyes darting back and forth across the cavernous room.

"Does this grand hall not look familiar?" Fitzwilliam asked.

"Of course it looks familiar," Jack snapped. "But *why* does it look familiar is the question we should be asking ourselves," he mumbled.

The walls were gilded, and the marble room was aglow with the light of hundreds of torches. It was all rather overwhelming.

"Wonder where everyone is?" Jack said. "Probably off giving thanks to good old Chantico for devouring us . . ."

"Jack, look at that wall," Fitzwilliam interrupted. "That is even more familiar yet. . . ."

Jack moved across the floor to take a closer look.

On the far wall, illuminated by torches, a large crest was engraved into the stone. He took another step closer and then he heard a soft, but distinct, click.

This was not good.

Suddenly, the floor rolled open under Jack's feet, and he and Fitzwilliam were plunged into a deep and seemingly endless pit.

CHAPTER NINE

*J*ack landed with a loud splash, followed by an equally loud splattering of water, indicating that Fitzwilliam had landed nearby. They were in a deep pool of what they could only *hope* was dirty water. Jack bobbed to the surface followed shortly thereafter by Fitzwilliam.

Like the main hall, the underground chamber they now found themselves in was lit by rows of torches. Fitzwilliam, sopping wet, stared at the equally soaked Jack.

"What?" Jack asked.

Fitzwilliam didn't say anything. He simply turned and swam to what looked like a shallow part of the pool. Out of the corner of his eye, Jack could have sworn he saw a large tail dip beneath the surface. He decided it must be his mind playing tricks on him. Although . . . the cavernous place they'd landed in did look eerily like the lair of the Merfolk—vicious mermaids who took pleasure only in driving people mad. He had experienced their not-so-pleasant company on one too many occasions.*

Not eager to find out if it was a mermaid, Jack quickly made his way over to Fitzwilliam. The aristocrat had climbed out of

*Most notably, Vol. 2, *The Siren Song*, and Vol. 4, *The Sword of Cortés*

the water and was now hanging his silk coat out to dry, emptying his shoes of water, and wringing out his stockings. He was also not even attempting to look at Jack.

"Hello," Jack said, waving a hand in front of Fitzwilliam's face.

Fitzwilliam just glared angrily.

"Not talking to me again?" Jack asked. "Thank you for that!"

Fitzwilliam put his hands over his face in dejected exasperation, and then leaned against the wall at his back. But instead of lending him the support he had expected to receive, the wall slid open just as the floor had earlier. With a groan, Fitzwilliam fell flat on his back. Tilting his head, he took in the surroundings. The moving wall had opened to reveal a long, narrow corridor. It was lit, as everything else was, by rows of torches.

"Better grab your things, Fitzy," Jack said, patting him on the shoulder. "Looks like you've just found us a way out."

The two boys carefully followed the length of the corridor. The ground was very muddy, making it difficult to walk. And, as neither of them were in any mood for idle chatter, all was silent save for their slushy footsteps.

"We have been walking for a least a half hour," Fitzwillaim complained, breaking the silence.

"A quarter hour at most," Jack said.

"Had I still been in possession of my watch, it would be easy to tell how long we had been traveling along this path," the aristocrat snapped.

"Yes, well," Jack said, trying to find a way to move the subject away from the watch he was hiding from Fitzwilliam. Luckily, he was saved from excuses by Fitzwilliam's next words.

"I am finding it difficult to move my legs."

"I find no humor in your pranks." Jack said. Then he grunted. It felt as though someone were pulling on his legs. "Um, Fitzy . . ."

"What?"

"Were you perhaps speaking just now of an odd sensation in your lower calves, which might feel like something is possibly preventing you from moving forward?"

"Genius! I wonder how you knew?"

"Let's just say that I am not having the easiest time moving either, savvy?"

Their eyes met in the torchlight.

"Jack, if I dare say it, you seem to be shrinking."

Jack looked down toward his feet. He couldn't see them. And he was seeing less and less of his legs as the seconds passed.

"Uh-oh," Jack said. "Quicksand!"

Fitz's eyes went wide with shock.

Jack, however, seemed less worried. In fact, he seemed downright calm. "Our standard Plan B—running—would not work in this situation," Jack pointed out. "Lucky for us, I have a backup." Smiling, Jack pulled Fitzwilliam's watch from his pocket.

"You! You told me that Jones was now in possession of my watch."

Jack shrugged, "Yes, well, I was not being entirely honest."

"You were not being honest at all!"

"Not so, Jones *had* been in possession of your watch for a brief time, before I secured it once again. So there was a good deal of truth in my so-called untruthful comment."

Even by the dim light of the torches, Jack could see Fitzwilliam's face turn beet red. Then the aristocrat launched into a screaming tirade against Jack, his voice reverberating in the hollow halls of the tunnel.

Jack just rolled his eyes and lifted the crown of the watch.

Silence. No more trickle of dripping water, no more echoing cavernous sounds, and best of all, no more annoying aristocrat.

"Now, to get me out of this sticky situation," Jack said. But when Jack tried to move his legs, his eyes grew wide. He was stuck! It seemed as though stopping time had made this particular situation worse. The quicksand had taken the consistency of cement without the passage of time there to move it along.

Jack sighed and started the watch ticking again. The corridor immediately filled with

the sound of Fitzwilliam's screaming. As before, it was clear he had not even realized that there had been a period during which time stood still.

"Are you done?" Jack said.

Fitzwilliam tried to kick in frustration, but as he couldn't move his legs, he only succeeded in straining a muscle in his thigh. "Ow!" he screamed, rubbing his leg and scowling indignantly at Jack.

Jack ignored Fitzwilliam's fit of rage. When the other boy was done yelping, Jack sighed deeply. "Fitzy—now is not the time for dramatics as I have a question of the most serious nature to pose—has your watch, in fact, always done this?"

"Done *what*?" Fitzwilliam shouted bitterly.

"This stopping-time thing?"

"I told you before, I have no bloody

idea what you are on about, Sparrow."

"Ahem," Jack cleared his throat. "Allow me to exhibit its strange and wonderful powers to you."

Jack once again lifted the crown from the watch and let out a laugh at Fitzwilliam's frozen expression—arms crossed, a twisted mix of angst, rage, and curiosity on his face.

Reaching over as far as he could, he began to write with his finger on the loose dirt path that lined the tunnel:

I WROTE THIS SENTENCE WHILE TIME WAS GOING ALL FUNNY. SAVVY?

Then Jack started the watch running again. Fitzwilliam did not notice what Jack had done right away. That is, until Jack opened his eyes wide and nodded his head toward the ground.

Upon seeing the note, Fitzwilliam's jaw dropped.

"The watch . . . it must have been charmed at some point, after it was taken from me." Fitzwilliam sputtered. "But how, and by whom? And how did it wind up in a pawn shop in New Orleans?"*

Before Jack and Fitzwilliam could take their conversation any further, a wet sound, like a carriage being drawn through slush by multiple horses, came from the far end of the corridor. And from that same direction, a strong light began to illuminate the tunnel,

*Fitz found his watch in New Orleans in Vol. 5, *The Age of Bronze*

casting shadows of what looked like some very tall men up on the wall.

"Quick!" Fitzwilliam said. "Use the watch!"

And without thinking, Fitz leaned over and grabbed the timepiece from Jack. The two boys fought for control of it, and with a sudden jerk (it wasn't clear who pulled hardest) the watch flew from the boys' hands and dropped into the quicksand.

Fitzwilliam swallowed hard.

Jack tilted his head and cocked an eyebrow as if to say, "now look what you've done."

And all the while, as the boys—and the watch—kept sinking, the figures at the end of the tunnel grew ever closer.

CHAPTER TEN

*B*efore Jack or Fitzwilliam could figure a way out of the insurmountable mess they found themselves in, a group of men appeared in front of them. They looked similar to those the duo had encountered earlier—Aztec clothing but clearly European features. They stood around Jack and Fitzwilliam on what was evidently the more stable portion of flooring in the cavern.

Before either of the boys could utter even a word of greeting, a familiar voice rang out.

"So, you have outwitted the gods. Chantico will not be pleased, nor am *I*." The head warrior, who had earlier condemned Jack and Fitzwilliam to death by becoming breakfast bacon for the goddess Chantico, had returned.

"Wow, you gentlemen do have a way of getting around this island. Neither I nor my crewmate here have had such luck. Might you want to think about selling maps to the tourists down by the docks? You'd make a killing. And I'd be happy to accept kickbacks . . ." Jack said.

"Silence!" the tribe leader demanded, and Jack straightened his back as best he could, given the circumstances. He was now waist-deep in the quicksand, as was Fitzwilliam.

"I could leave you here to sink beneath the sand," the leader said.

Fitzwilliam tried to keep a brave expression

on his face, but it was clear he was beginning to think that there might be no way out of this one. After all that he and Jack had been through, it seemed this really could be the end.

"Now what would be the fun in that?" Jack asked bravely.

"My sentiments exactly," the leader said.

Fitzwilliam let out a sigh and his expression relaxed—a moment too soon.

"I think allowing you to drown here would be far too lenient. Men, throw each of these interlopers a line."

Two of the warriors quickly unraveled lengths of rope that hung at their waists like lassos. One guard tossed a rope to Jack, and another to Fitzwilliam. Fitzwilliam looked questioningly at Jack. Had he not been so terrified, he might have been able to ask if it was a wise idea to take the rope. But

Jack never did need to hear a question to answer it.

"Well, we have two options," Jack said. "Either we stay here and drown, or we're pulled out by these Brits who think they're Aztecs, and die a painful death on a volcano or the gallows or a spit somewhere."

"That does not present us with many options, does it?"

"Not many pleasant ones," Jack conceded. "But as long as we're out of this sandpit, there's at least *some* hope."

Shrugging at Jack's questionable logic, Fitzwilliam grabbed the rope. The warrior on the other end let out a grunt, and in the blink of an eye, Fitzwilliam found himself on the solid ground that surrounded the quicksand.

Jack, however, hesitated for a moment, his hand hovering over the rope. Something had caught his eye. There was a very faint glint coming from the sand. Jack squinted to try to make out exactly what it was. Then he smiled. It was a bit of the chain from Fitzwilliam's watch! It wasn't completely submerged yet!

Checking to make sure Fitzwilliam wasn't paying attention, Jack reached out his hand. But it was no use. His torso was far too submerged to allow for any movement. Grabbing the rope in one hand for support, Jack leaned out farther. But the warrior on the other end of the rope took that as a sign that Jack was ready to be removed from the sand. He began to pull.

From where he stood, Fitzwilliam couldn't figure out why Jack seemed to be upset that the tribe was pulling him *out* of the pit. Hadn't he just stated that it would be better out of the sand than in it? Fitz sighed. There was no point in trying to figure out Jack.

Meanwhile, the warrior gave another quick tug and Jack felt like he was going to be ripped apart. Pulling Fitzwilliam out had been easy. But that was because Fitzwilliam was not resisting. Jack, however, was not leaving until he had that watch.

Another warrior grabbed the rope and the men tugged again. Jack was pulled out far enough to be submerged only from the calves down. He sighed in frustration. One more tug, and the watch would be lost forever. Given the circumstances, Jack could not let that happen. If there was any way to get off the island alive, he'd need that watch to do it.

Now there were three men, plus Fitz-william, tugging on the rope to hoist Jack out. They gave one, great, final tug and Jack came completely free of the sand. But as they dragged Jack out, he noticed something that felt like seaweed catch around his ankle.

He looked down toward his boots. He was indeed a lucky fellow. . . . He'd managed to grab the watch with his boot at the decisive moment!

"You know, I was beginning to like it in there," Jack said, attempting to cover up his true intentions for wanting to stay in the pit. "It was not unlike those mud baths I hear so much about queens and countesses enjoying. If you could have given me two cucumber slices for my eyes, I would have been in *heaven!*"

"Enough," the leader demanded. "Men, take them to the throne room."

"You've got your own throne? And still, you're slumming it down here with the rest of us common folk? Well, my opinion of you has certainly shifted, my greatness. A true man of the people you are, if I do say so myself," Jack said, ending with a bow.

"The throne is not mine."

"That's a pity," Jack said. "I knew it was too much to ask for a leader who would get down and dirty in the mud with his warriors. Oh, well."

With a nod from the man who was clearly no longer the leader, the guards pushed Jack and Fitzwilliam forward and began to march them down another long corridor.

As he walked, Jack was very conscious of the watch around his ankle. At any moment, the ticking device could slip off. Not to mention that the watch was making a jingling sound with every step Jack took. Thankfully, the warriors' marching feet drowned out the sound well enough.

A few minutes later, they arrived at a large cage. The guards quickly tied Jack's and Fitzwilliam's hands again, and tossed the boys—quite rudely, Jack thought—inside.

Jack's heart raced as the violent shove sent the watch into a fit of jingling. But it did not fall off, and the guards remained unaware.

"You mates really like locking fellows up, don't you?" Jack asked, hoping to keep the attention from the watch around his ankle.

The guards, and the man who Jack previously thought was the tribe leader, sneered silently at Jack. And then something strange started to happen. The men began to sink beneath Jack and Fitzwilliam. Could it be more quicksand?

"Huh?" Jack said.

Then Jack realized it wasn't the men who were sinking, it was Jack and Fitzwilliam who were *rising*. The cage they'd been thrown in was being hoisted up into a chamber above them.

"Wow," Jack said, "this place really is at

the height of engineering. Get it, 'height'?" Jack smiled.

Fitzwilliam, for his part, seemed to be back in not-speaking-to-Jack mode.

When the elevator arrived at the top, the gate was thrown open by two beautiful girls.

"Thank you, madams," Jack said, smiling, his gold tooth glinting in the torchlight.

Despite the dire circumstances, the girls smiled back, and the cuter of the two even winked at him.

"Can't resist my charm," Jack whispered to Fitzwilliam. Then he turned to the cute girl. "Let's talk when this is all through, savvy?" Jack said, winking back at her.

At the far end of the chamber, a man sat on a throne, his body lost in the shadows cast by the flickering torchlight.

"Bring them forward," he said, in a deep, gravelly voice.

The women grabbed Jack and Fitzwilliam by their bound hands (the one Jack was flirting with was quick to escort him) and walked them toward the man on the throne.

He cut a very striking—not to mention intimidating—figure. His black hair was slicked down over his left eye. He wore a bandana, and his fingers, neck, and ears were adorned with jewels. His eyes were lined with kohl, and his teeth had been frightfully shaved into points, so it looked as though he had a mouth full of fangs. From his getup, this man appeared to be a pirate, and a dangerous one at that—what with legions of warriors on the island to protect him.

"Kneel," the pirate said when the two boys were in front of him.

"No, offense, mate, but Jack Sparrow kneels for no—"

But before Jack could finish, the cute girl,

still smiling sheepishly, kicked Jack in the back of the knees, and he fell to the ground before the fearsome pirate. Fitzwilliam, who had also been resisting, was taken down in a similar fashion by his own escort.

"I like a girl who packs a punch," Jack said, half smiling, half agonizing. "We really do need to talk."

"Leave us," the pirate told the girls. "But first, sever their ties so that when I kill them, they can't say I didn't play fair."

The girls bowed, whipping out daggers and swiftly cutting the ties that bound Jack and Fitzwilliam. Jack shook his hands free and blew his girl a kiss. She smiled and then retreated back to the far end of the chamber along with her cohort.

For a brief second, as the girls retreated and the pirate looked on, Jack thought he might be able to bend down and grab the watch, which was still wrapped around his boot. But he did not end up having enough time, for the frightening pirate stood up, his sword drawn. Jack would have to wait for the right moment before snagging the watch.

"So, you were able to defeat the goddess Chantico," the vile man hissed. "Or, perhaps, she freed you herself. After all, the heathen gods have no love lost for me. If you ask me, I think they're just jealous."

The pirate was now leaning in close to Jack and Fitzwilliam, his rotten teeth reeking in his foul mouth.

"But, just because you were able to free yourselves from a goddess," he continued, "does not mean you'll be able to escape me— I, who am more powerful than a god. Boys, prepare to meet your maker—at the hands of Stone-Eyed Sam and his all powerful weapon, the Sword of Cortés!"

CHAPTER ELEVEN

$\mathcal{J}$ack and Fitzwilliam stood before the vicious pirate—a pirate who should not have been there at all—in a state of shock.

"Sorry, mate, but you can't be Stone-Eyed Sam," Jack said. "He's dead. We saw his skeleton. And that's not the Sword of Cortés in your hand. The sword—if you must know, even though I probably should not be telling you such classified information—is with the powerful mystic Tia Dalma for safekeeping."*

*Jack and his crew handed the dangerous weapon over to Tia Dalma in Vol. 4, the *Sword of Cortés*

The pirate smirked, pointed his sword at the ceiling, and turned a huge stalactite into a slithering boa constrictor.

"Oh," Jack said, recognizing the Sword's power. "Yeah, that's the Sword of Cortés all right."

"I am glad you have come to realize the truth. You were lucky to have survived my small army. All good sailors, charmed by the sword into believing they are Aztec warriors and that I am a god. I would do the same to you—turn you into my servants—were you more fit." Jack winced at this insult. "Now prepare to meet your fate!" Stone-Eyed Sam shouted. Then, he lunged at the boys, the Sword glowing powerfully with sparks and flames.

"Yikes!" Jack said, jumping away quickly.

At that very moment, Fitzwilliam noticed the watch, dangling from Jack's boot.

"Jack! The watch!"

Jack was so flustered with all this Stone-Eyed Sam business, that he had all but forgotten that he had retrieved the watch. Before he could do anything, Fitzwilliam lunged for the timepiece and tried to grab its chain.

But there was no way Jack was about to let go of the watch and its power. Reaching down, he closed his fingers on the chain and held on tightly. Then, as a confused Stone-Eyed Sam looked on, the two boys tugged at the timepiece.

Finally, Jack managed to lift the crown and everything went still—except for Jack . . . and, this time, Fitzwilliam. . . .

"You were not kidding, then?" Fitzwilliam said. "It stops time—literally?"

"No, I was not kidding, then," Jack said.

"I dare say that I am somewhat confused

by the goings-on here," Fitzwilliam said.

"What's not clear to you, mate?" Jack said. "Now we know why this island and that temple looked familiar to us. We've even been down that booby-trapped floor before. We're in Stone-Eyed Sam's pirate kingdom on *Isla Esquelética*. And we're somehow here *before* he lost his all-powerful Sword and fell from power."*

"Right, Jack. That makes *so* much sense. You said yourself that Sam was dead. We saw his remains. We delivered the Sword to Tia Dalma ourselves," Fitzwilliam argued.

"These points all raise questions. You shouldn't open your mouth unless you have answers, too, savvy?"

"I *did* notice Sam's mark in that grand hall. I just didn't think too much of it. He

*The first time they escaped the island was back in Vol. 1, *The Coming Storm*

could have left his mark in a lot of places,"
Fitzwilliam admitted. "But he had been dead
for years by the time we first visited his
island. His kingdom was in ruins. If this is
the same place, does it mean he has been res-
urrected? And that his city has somehow
risen from the ashes as well?"

Jack and Fitzwilliam looked back at the
terrifying—but frozen—pirate. His fanglike
teeth were bared, and the huge X of a scar
that marked his face was red with rage.

Turning from the pirate, Jack looked
down at the watch again.

"I gather that we're both still moving
despite time having stopped, because you
were touching the watch chain when I lifted
the crown out and stopped it," Jack said.
"Since we both have all the time in the
world, let's try to find our way out of this
place."

Now that Jack and Fitzwilliam knew for certain that they had been in this temple before, they looked around eagerly, hoping to see something that would guide them out. But it wasn't that easy. The last time Jack and Fitzwilliam had been in this throne room, it had been a dilapidated mess. There had been none of the splendor that it possessed here and now.

Suddenly, Jack remembered that there had been an opening right over Sam's throne. He had always thought it was there because the throne room had fallen into disrepair. But with all the trapdoors and hidden passageways, he wondered if Sam had put an escape hatch there intentionally. Nodding at Fitz to follow, Jack made his way over to the throne.

Pulling himself up, Jack stood on top of it. Sure enough, there was a rope ladder leading up to the roof of the chamber, and beyond,

Jack could see sunlight. Bowing, Jack motioned to Fitzwilliam.

"Ladies first," Jack said, smiling.

Fitzwilliam sneered but did not forfeit the opportunity to escape the terrifying chamber. Shimmying up quickly, he disappeared from sight. Once again, the room was quiet, save for Jack's breathing. Fitzwilliam made not a peep.

"Mighty quiet up there, mate," Jack pointed out as he climbed up the ladder himself.

When he got to the top, he realized just why Fitzwilliam had been speechless. Above them, filling the sky, still as everything else in the world, were what looked like huge birds. Bigger—and stranger—than any birds Jack had ever seen. They were leathery, not feathered, with huge beaks, and their wings stretched for what looked like fifty feet.

"Wow—lots of birds. Flying north for

the summer, you think?" Jack asked.

"Jack," Fitzwilliam answered, "These are pterodactyls. They were largely thought to be a thing of legend, but I have a tutor who claims to have uncovered the bones of just such an animal. He also claims that they went extinct millions of years ago. Jack, this watch—I don't think it's just *stopping* time . . ."

". . . It's making it go all funny," Jack finished for Fitzwilliam. "That certainly explains why Stone-Eyed Sam's kingdom is still intact. And why the *Barnacle*'s skiff was missing and there was a totem pole in its place. The skiff must have been carved from a totem pole, and when I used the watch, it reverted to that state."

"What do you propose we do now?" Fitzwilliam asked sincerely, for once.

"For someone who loves to incessantly mock my status as captain, you certainly do ask a lot of advice of me," Jack snarled. "Nevertheless we will try to make our way back to the *Barnacle*, and see if there's some way to sail away from this horrid *island—again*. . . ."*

With a clear view of the entire island, the boys quickly found a path from the jungle to the shore. Running away from the temple at top speed, they burst through the foliage to find the *Barnacle* still there, but . . .

"Looks like reboarding the boat is out of the question. Unless we want to face Davy Jones again," Jack said breathlessly.

The *Flying Dutchman* was docked just yards from the *Barnacle*, surely awaiting Jack and Fitzwilliam's return.

"So, let us take stock. We have Jones in the water, extinct flying beasts in the sky

*Jack and his crew first visited the island in Vol. 1, *The Coming Storm*

overhead, and Stone-Eyed Sam and the powerfully evil Sword of Cortés on the land behind us. And we already know what is under our feet—booby traps and sandpits. I ask again, what do we do now?" Fitzwilliam said.

"We stay here," Jack said proudly. "We fight. And once we defeat Sammy and his strange mock Aztecs, we make our way onto the *Barnacle*, and give it our best shot against Jones."

"Why not just find our skiff and sail to another island," Fitzwilliam asked.

"Oh, Fitzy," Jack said. "You obviously don't remember the last time we were here. This island is in the middle of *nowhere*! We'd never make it to another island before we starved to death or died of exhaustion! And if we're caught out at sea—it's Jones's Locker for us both."

The odds seemed insurmountable. But Fitzwilliam realized there was likely no other way out of this situation. The only thing the boys had in their favor was the watch. And that was very likely what had gotten them into this mess in the first place. This would probably be the trickiest, possibly deadliest, fight of their lives.

"Ready?" Jack said.

"As I will ever be," Fitzwilliam said.

The boys nodded to one another, and with a steely resolve, they set off to win back their lives, their boat, and most important of all, their freedom.

To be continued . . .

Don't miss the next volume in the continuing adventures of Jack Sparrow and the crew of the mighty Barnacle*!*

Dance of the Hours

Jack and Fitzwilliam are stuck on an island full of possessed sailors who think they are Aztecs and a pirate king they believed to be dead, while Davy Jones waits for them out at sea. All they are armed with is a mystical timepiece that seems to be more trouble than its worth. Will Jack and Fitz be able to escape all these threats, *plus* what might be their most dangerous adversary ever—the goddess Chantico?